GODS' MAN

A NOVEL IN WOODCUTS BY LYND WARD

St. Martin's Press, Inc.
175 Fifth Avenue
New York, N.Y. 10010

Library of Congress Cataloging in Publication Data

Ward, Lynd Kendall, 1905-
  Gods' man.

1. Ward, Lynd Kendall, 1905-   2. Stories without words.   I. Title.
II. Title: A novel in woodcuts.
NE1112.W37A4   1978   769'.92'4   77-91889
ISBN 0-312-33100-2 (cloth)
ISBN 0-312-33101-0 (paper)

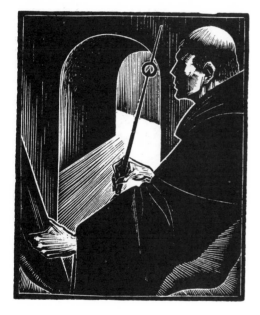 

THE MISTRESS

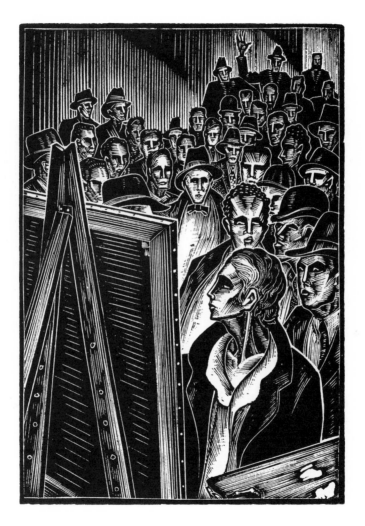

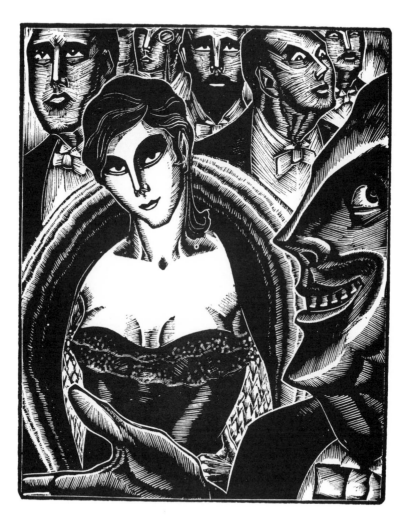

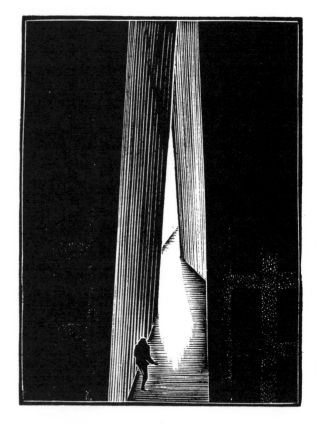

IV.
THE
WIFE

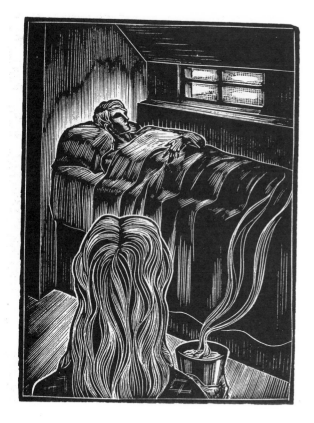

V.
THE
PORTRAIT